Almost Never

Teresa Adele Bettino

Cover Photo: Nancy and Edward Bettino, Sr.
Back Cover Photo: Courtesy Janet Frascella Morris

Cover Design: Sherry Ferrell

Although this work is based on a true event, this
novel is a work of fiction. This true event
happened to my father, Edward Thomas Bettino,
Sr. however; this author has woven fact and fiction.
Names, descriptions, entities and incidents
included in this story are products of this author's
imagination.

ISBN: 978-0-9742842-6-2

Sherry Ferrell is Teresa Adele Bettino's editor and friend. She is also the founder and sole proprietor of Fer-Sher Publishing, established in 2006 with the release of *Primary Concerns,* which describes Sherry's journey to better health. Sherry is actively involved with the publishing process; editing content and designing book covers. Mrs. Ferrell's designs can be seen at: http://book-cover-designer.blogspot.com/

Sherry is pleased to announce *Almost Never* is the fifth of Teresa Adele Bettino's books published by Fer-Sher Publishing.

Dedication

To my father, Edward Thomas Bettino, Sr. -
La Speranza

And uncle, Albert Bettino- La Memoria

Special thoughts

Adele Gondolfo-Il Cuore

Anna Mumola-Il Gioiello

Nancy Helen Bettino-La Montagna

Celeste Bettino and Edward Thomas
Bettino, Jr. - Molto Tempo Fa

Photo: Edward Thomas Bettino, Sr. and brother, Albert Bettino

A Soldier's Aloneness

For dad

A veteran sits on a beach

Staring at waves

Lapping onto sand

A cool breeze intermingles

Touching his skin

Gently embracing his body.

His battle ended years ago

Ever present within

Flashbacks always bring panic

Tranquility of the moment

Engulfs his being

With a gentle rhythm.

Almost Never

Teresa Adele Bettino

1

The gentle rocking of my great-grandmother's chair, throughout the day, was her familiar dance, as she moved with cadence amid the passage of days, weeks and years. This tempo of life mixed with today's rain as it splashed upon a nearby windowsill seemed to comfort her in a small way.

Nana's sun porch with its many windows and plants had an earthy smell. A repotted Crown of Thorns plant placed underneath an open window facing Columbus Avenue is what I remember on this day. Her Crown of Thorns cared for since the Depression of 1929, its stretched branches pointed upwards, appeared thirsty as water splashed from the windowpane, in rhythm with Nana's rocking.

As Nana rocked she held a piece of paper, yellowed by age. Nana removed her glasses, wiped her eyes with an ironed handkerchief hidden inside the breast area of her dress. Gently patting her warm salty tears, Nana gathered her rosary and made the Sign of the Cross. She nodded her head and said, "Quasi mai."

"Why are you crying?"

"I remember my grandson."

"What do you remember?"

"World War II, it's about your great-grandfather, so many years ago."

"What does quasi mai mean, Nana?"

"It means, almost never."

"Why does quasi mai make you sad?"

"Life is almost never. Life with your great-grandfather was almost never."

"But Nana, great-grandfather lived a long time. He was old when he died."

"Yes, my grandson. Your nonno lived a full life. He lived each day happily."

Folks speak of moments within their lives and for me this day is one of them. My great-grandfather, whom I called Nonno, a gentle man with blue eyes and a warm smile, made my Nana very happy and contented. He made me the man I am today.

On this dreary rainy New Jersey day, I stare at a polished hardwood floor gathering rings of rainwater surrounding Nana's beloved Crown of Thorns.

"Can I sit on your lap, Nana?"

"Certo...of course."

Nana lifts me onto her lap. I lay my head onto her bosom listening to her heart. With the unison of rain and heart, we fall asleep. Nana holding me with her left arm across my waist, clutching her handkerchief and in her right hand a white rosary, with one bead secured between her thumb and index finger moving with progression. We dream as one. We travel back in time.

Multicolored rose petals swirl on Trenton Rail Station's black and white tile floor as a door slams and pigeons take flight. I watch as red and white petals lift into the air, startled by the wind of pigeons. I suck my thumb, watching this movie...this dream, while Nana moves her rocker, back and forth. Our breathing becomes one as does our reality.

I see the eyes of frantic pigeons as they smash against the train station's windows, causing cracks and splatters of blood. I'm drawn deeper into sleep. Nana's rosary beads come to my fingers and I begin to roll one bead at a time. I move my eyes away from pigeons and see Nana, as a young woman.

An attractive woman, with Mediterranean skin, brown curly thick hair, hazel eyes with wire glasses; dressed in a bright blue dress, clutching a black leather pocketbook. She sits on a wooden bench. I see a Trenton newspaper, next to her... February 14, 1944.

Nana seems nervous, as she rubs her hands and her thumbs intertwine making circles. Her thumbs move quickly, around and around as a pigeon walks close to her pecking tiles. Her pocketbook sits on her lap.

A train is announced. Nana opens her pocketbook and removes a white piece of notepaper. She makes the Sign of the Cross and stands. Travelers, mostly soldiers exit the train. There's excitement within this station. Nana stands, searching; her eyes moving wildly through the crowded station. She watches. Nobody comes to her. She returns the white piece of notepaper to her pocketbook, snapping it shut and begins to leave.

A woman dressed in black with a colorful apron, approaches Nana. She's holding roses. I hear the rose lady say, "Quasi mai...almost never," as she walks along side of Nana. I take it from her expression that she knows my great-grandmother.

The rose lady walks with Nana to another bench and the women sit. She pats Nana's hand and from the pockets of her apron offers Nana red and white rose petals. She gestures to scatter the petals onto the floor. "Be done with it," she says.

"I won't be done with it. My husband will return from war, like others."

The rose lady scatters more petals. She takes a handful of breadcrumbs and feeds pigeons.

"It breaks my heart to see you wait...day after day...week after week...a year already?"

"Eddie was inducted into the Army, April, 1943. At least when he was at Camp Dix, I was within reach." Nana says, removing her glasses as she dabs her eyes.

"Today, Valentine's Day, almost one year and you don't know where he is?

"No. I have one letter that I read every day."

Pigeons scurry about Nana's feet. The rose lady throws a few more petals and crumbs.

"Be done with it" she says getting to her feet and walking away.

A shoeshine man, dressed in a tattered suit, too large for his small frame, joins Nana. He takes a seat where the rose lady has been. He stares at breadcrumbs and rose petals on the black and white tile floor. Nana looks into his eyes, he tries to smile. She tearfully says, "Quasi mai."

"Don't listen to the rose lady. She's old and superstitious."

"I know. She's old world. I have plenty of time to wait for my Eddie."

"And he will come one day through those doors."

The shoeshine man and Nana depart. He returns to his spot near the door at South Clinton Avenue and Nana leaves Trenton Rail Station walking along Greenwood Avenue. She cries as she strolls home.

2

I travel on this Valentine's Day to Italy, a little south of Aprilia, not far from the beaches of Anzio. A handsome young man, with crystal blue eyes, light brown hair and an athletic build, is standing in front of his commanding officer listening to orders. He appears cold, and rubs his eyes as a child that's tired, although; he listens intently. The officer pats him on his back and he salutes, turns, and abruptly leaves his regiment behind.

He walks through several large fields and locates an American command post. He salutes the commanding officer, "Sir, more ammunition and reinforcements are needed immediately."

"Private, tell your commanding officer that we're doing what we can. We know your location."

Eddie's dismissed. Friendly fire is heard overhead as Eddie walks swiftly with purpose through several fields lined with tall sea grasses. Eddie's hands are cold; knuckles white, as he holds them in front of his mouth blowing warm air onto them. His frozen nostrils are uncomfortable, making breathing painful. He takes short breaths as he journeys.

Eddie nervously scours his area checking in front, to his sides and behind. The noise of background mortar fire, a constant reminder of war, resonates with smoke lines within the gray sky. An American soldier hiding within the grasses stands suddenly and motions Eddie to join him. Eddie hadn't seen him. This action unnerves him. The soldier grabs Eddie's arm in an attempt to have Eddie join him. "Who are you? Where's your company?" Eddie whispers.

"The German's wiped us out...I'm the only one left."

"Walk with me as I'm returning to American lines. I'm with the 45th Infantry

Division. I've just given the post commander a message from my commanding officer that additional ammunition and reinforcements are necessary to secure our position. The Nazi's have us surrounded."

"Man, there's not many left. It's you and me. What's your name?"

"What? It's hard to hear with all of the mortar fire."

"Your name, man."

"Eddie Bettino. Yours?"

Machine gun fire sprays the field. Eddie's shot in both legs. He holds his hands onto his legs and realizes that he's been hit with machine gun fire. Blood seeps onto his pant legs. Pain encompasses his shaking body. Dazed he begins to crawl as gunfire continues to rip through the field. His traveling companion scrambles to Eddie, picks him up and begins running through the field carrying his wounded comrade over his shoulder. He comes to where a command post was and now is no longer as American forces have retreated.

"Eddie, man...I'm gonna have to leave you. I'll leave you here. Try to hide in the grass. Man, I hate doing this, but I've got to move quicker. I'll return with some help."

The soldier bends from the waist and carefully lowers Eddie's bloody body.

"Eddie, listen to me. Here's my canteen, a few candy bars and a couple of cigarettes and a matchbook. I'll be back, I promise."

"What's your name?"

The soldier breathes deeply eyeing Eddie's wounds. He takes a moment and wipes tears from his eyes and holds Eddie's hand. "Eddie, stay with me man, I'm Norman Kauffman from the Bronx. I promise that I won't leave you here. I'll return."

Nana's wool coat is buttoned and a silk green kerchief covers her head shielding her from February's damp cold. With drawn shoulders, Nana removes her handkerchief from her coat pocket stopping to wipe her eyes. She stands by a barren Maple Tree, holds onto the tree's trunk, removes her glasses and weeps. She spends moments weeping. I watch as Nana looks up to the sky. She wipes her eyes, blows her nose and returns her handkerchief to her left pocket as if she has been given direction or resignation. Her hands join her coat pockets. With wind spinning flakes of snow mixed with sleet, Nana trudges home.

Blood seeps from Eddie's injuries saturating his uniform. He lies in the grass, knowing that his comrade will not return and is overcome by physical and mental despair. His body shivers from shock and loss of blood. *I'm just nineteen* he says, as he drifts into unconsciousness. Speckles of snow begin to fall. In the distance, I hear sounds of guns firing. German tanks move closer to Nonno.

Eddie awakens. He shakes his head and attempts to move his feet. His pants are drenched with blood mixed with skin and muscle. Desperate to find American lines, he begins crawling. Eddie claws his fingers into the ground dragging his bloody useless legs behind. A trail of blood mixes with sandy soil as German soldiers follow and spot Eddie. A husky German picks him up throwing Eddie over his shoulder like a sack of potatoes. The German says in broken English, "For you, the war is over." The squad delivers Eddie to a field shack, opposite American lines.

This field shack, dark and cold; smells of bowels, urine, blood and fear. American, British and some Australian soldiers moan in unison, withering in pain, grief and despair. With a combination of American and German artillery firing overhead, relentlessly causing much stress to the compound, this primitively constructed shack takes a direct hit from allied shelling. Bodies within become missiles as men are thrown, tossed about. Body parts fly throughout the shack as Eddie's knocked across the structure onto a wall. There's bedlam within and outside. Eddie spots the shack's open door, decides to flee, and slowly makes his way outside, hopeful for freedom.

Chaos surrounds Eddie. Many German bodies are strewn around the compound. He crawls over a dead German, takes his winter coat, throws it over his back and continues creeping, crawling and clawing his way along a frozen dirt road. Blood flows profusely from massive leg injuries; his mutilated left leg collects dirt within machine gun holes.

With a mixture of unbearable pain and adrenaline, Eddie slowly inches his way to American lines. An hour, two hours pass, as freezing rain commences causing the

German coat to saturate Eddie's back. It's now heavier becoming stiff as the temperature falls. Eddie's finger- nails split upward drawing pain and blood within his fingers as he continues this journey, a passage through hell.

3

Nana arrives to her small apartment. It's cold inside. She conserves the use of electricity and oil by not turning lights on and lowering her heat. There's not much money for rent, bills and food without Eddie.

She shuffles through her bedroom, locating her flashlight and goes to the back of the flat, still carrying her pocket book. The kitchen's bleak. There's little food. Nana lights the gas stove's pilot light, places a pot of water on the range, waits for the water to boil and tosses a tea bag into the pot.

Her mind is elsewhere. She rubs her temples in a circular motion and sits staring outside. She places her flash light on the table, lowers her head and begins crying. The rapid boiling of water causes the tea bag to move roughly within the pot. Nana lifts her head, pushes her chair from the table, gets up, and walks to the stove. She pours hot water with a tea bag into an old chipped light blue mug. Nana returns to the table. She watches the water darken, as her mood mixes with this dreary day and murky tea. Nana takes a photo of a young soldier from her pocketbook. It's of a young soldier, with a wide smile.

This photo, remains within my heart. I see you all day, every day. It's like looking at the black and white train station tiles. They're ever present. Every day I come, go to work and return to the train station waiting...am I to wait my life for you? I study your smile, your blue eyes and handsome face. Your smiling face with your upper lip a bit off center shows your perfect smile. I study your slightly crooked nose, broken from boxing. I desire to touch you and kiss you, my Eddie. Where are you? Why don't I receive mail? I want you home. I remember when we had this photo taken. You had made an icy snowball, gathering the snow from the side of the cobbled stone road, near Broad Street and threw it to me in your fun-loving way. It's been a year...I didn't want you to go.   Life is short, although is long without you, my love.

Nana, places the photo onto the kitchen table, takes a swig of tea, and rests her head upon the table.   *What's happened? Where are you?*

We were high school sweethearts with our lives before us, with dreams.   You, always fun loving, energized, filled with life. And me, loving you since grade school, going to church with you and wanting nothing more than the security of your being...your soul and my grandmother's quilt on a rainy, snowy day such as; today. War...brutto.

Nana returns Eddie's photograph and takes a white crisp paper neatly folded from her pocketbook. Tears form in her eyes as a tear moves down her cheek onto her chin and inside the mug, chipped as her heart.

Quasi mai, Eddie...our life is it almost never? I will return tomorrow, sit on the bench waiting for you to return, my love.

A German troop wagon maneuvers on the road, moving to and fro. The driver stops and points, to Eddie. He's lying on the side of the road, a drenched frozen German coat covering him. One soldier jumps from the wagon, slings Eddie over his shoulder placing him in the back of the wagon. *They think that he's a comrade. I see my nonno being cared for by Germans and it looks like he's arriving at an Italian emergency hospital; it's surrounded by large boulders upon a mountain.*

The wagon bumps along a rocky dirt road heading towards Monte Cassino, where there are a few prison hospitals overcrowded with injured soldiers. Eddie's taken from the wagon, is carried into the hospital and placed onto a table. The

German soldier quickly exits without exchanging words.

An Italian surgeon and Maria, an Italian Red Cross nurse, remove Eddie's coat. It's wet and has frozen blood on it. The sleeve is tattered from being dragged through rough terrain. The medical doctor and nurse stare at raw legs, machine gun holes and infection. The doctor shakes his head.

The surgeon closes the room's door as the nurse removes Eddie's clothing. She speaks under her breath in Italian, *angelo*.

"His left leg needs to be amputated."

"Si."

"There's infection and he's lost much blood. He will need a transfusion."

"Look how young he's a, ragazzo... boy."

Maria makes the Sign of the Cross, as the surgeon begins with the amputation. She stands close, handing instruments to the doctor. She observes. Maria begins a blood transfusion, not knowing Eddie's blood type. She says a prayer to Saint Anthony, the saint of miracles. Again she makes the Sign of the Cross, holding her palms upward looking towards the ceiling as freezing rain pelts onto the roof of this emergency hospital. After the amputation, Maria holds Eddie's cold, lifeless hands. She speaks tenderly to Eddie. She prays.

Eddie struggles for life, each breath an effort. The medial doctor studies his right leg.

"Mio Dio...my God...not his right?" Maria says.

"Maria, this is not something that I take lightly. He may need the right taken too."

"No. Please wait. He's too weak...too young...my God...bambino."

The surgeon shakes his head back and forth. Beads of sweat dribble from his forehead. The doctor removes debris from Eddie's right leg, "I think with some luck, we may be able to save this right one, although it's pretty mangled."

Maria nods, helps with cleaning, stitching, and dressing Eddie's wounds. She continues to pray daily as she attends to other injured prisoners and Eddie. She hopes...hopes for Eddie and hopes for this war to end.

Three weeks later, Eddie has a high fever, marked with delirium. He isn't eating and is dehydrated. The surgeon removes the bandage on Eddie's right leg. It has a foul odor and is oozing.

"Maria, Eddie's right leg needs to be amputated if we are to save his life."

"I can't bare this. It's too much. So many young men injured, losing limbs and life."

"I know, however; we must do the best job that we can in miserable conditions. Eddie needs this amputation; gas gangrene has set in."

She makes the Sign of the Cross, "Jesus, Mary and Joseph have mercy on my Eddie," as she aides with Eddie's surgery.

Hours later when Maria has returned to her barren room within the hospital, she looks from her small window seeing the sun set above the mountaintops. Maria curses Mussolini; she curses Hitler raising her fist to the sky in anger as dusk begins. Exhausted from the day, Maria draws a curtain across her window, finds a washcloth to bathe the day's stress from her tired body.

Once completed, Maria holds her rosary as she pulls the sheets down within her single iron bed. Maria prays for the war to end, she prays for injured soldiers, she prays for guidance and safety of family and falls asleep holding her beads.

4

The sun shines through white cotton curtains in Nana's bedroom on this crisp February morning. Nana doesn't want to leave the warmth of her bed. She eyes the clock. It's five...*too early to rise for work...another half hour.* Nana covers her head with a heavy comforter and holds Eddie's pillow. She hasn't washed his pillowcase and won't until he returns.

When she closes her eyes and takes a deep breath she smells Eddie, his scent fills her. Nana falls back to sleep and dreams of Trenton Rail Station. There's the shoeshine man, who's waiting on a customer, busily cleaning and buffing his shoes. There's the rose lady near the bench, cutting rose stems and removing wilted petals. Pigeons are flocking to her, waiting for some breadcrumbs. Nana hears the rose lady say,

"Buongiorno," to everybody walking by. Nana sees herself as she walks by her friends. She doesn't answer to buongiorno. Instead she hangs her head, walks by the shoeshine man and rose lady quickly, ignoring them as she takes her seat on the station's bench. Nana places her pocket book on her knees and sits with interlaced fingers, twirling her thumbs, waiting.

A train arrives. Nana removes the folded paper from her pocket book, reads it and watches as passengers arrive. She returns the paper and snaps her pocket book shut. The rose lady arrives and takes a seat. She pats my grandmother's hand. The shoeshine man ambles over. Dried petals are handed to Nana. "Be done with it," the rose lady says while the shoeshine man nods. Nana cries. "I can't be done with it. He's my husband, my life."

The rose lady stands, throws petals onto the black and white tile floor, "He may never come. It's been over a year."

"I can't give up. I must wait for him."

The shoeshine man stands behind Nana. "Someday, Eddie will walk from the tracks, up these stairs and will greet you. I believe. There's hope that he will."

The rose lady throws a few crumbs to the pigeons. "Life's tricky. What will be will be! Be done with it and move on. You have your life ahead."

"I won't be done with it, until the bitter end." Nana says as she stands and flees from the station.

Mules carry supplies, men and artillery throughout mountainous Monte Cassino. Soldiers fight freezing conditions with little winter clothing. Some freeze in foxholes. High winds with sleet covers mules' fur forming icicles as they climb and slip their way up rocky terrain. The war continues around the hospital. Injured men arrive daily.

Maria tends to those injured. Eddie's severely ill and may die. The gas gangrene coupled with lack of medical supplies, along with malnourishment has jeopardized his life. He's semiconscious as Maria force-feeds Eddie liquids attempting to fend dehydration and fever.

She prays and sings Italian songs to Eddie tending to his care. Many soldiers are as Eddie. Her pleas to Saint Anthony are hourly. Her appeal for help strong, *My Saint Anthony, saint of hopelessness and miracles please have mercy on this young man. He doesn't know about his legs. Please spare his life, so that he may continue on his life's journey.*

During the night, Eddie awakens. He doesn't know where he is. There's a frown on his face as the room's dark. He hears moaning and smells disinfectant. Eddie feels around. He touches his face, his hair and feels his heart. His hands move further under stiff linens to his thighs. Eddie's stomach begins to ache. He slowly moves his hands to his knees. There's a stump below each knee. *Oh my God...no...I'm just nineteen. What am I to do? Where am I? This can't be, not so, I can't live like this. What's happened to me?* He cries.

Maria begins her shift at five in the morning. She helps the sick and injured take sponge baths and changes sheets. Breakfast, although scant will be made around seven. Maria sings as she enters Eddie's room. She looks to his bed and sees his eyes peeping from the sheet. She can't believe that Eddie's awake.

Eddie doesn't know who Maria is. He begins to cry. He's trying desperately to remember where he is and what's happened.

"Where am I and who are you?"

Maria replies in broken English. "Italy."

Eddie stares around the room. He spends a moment deep in thought. He speaks in Italian.

Eddie begins recalling his circumstance. Enormous emotional pain grips his heart. Maria attempts to console him.

"I want to die. Leave me alone!"

Maria leaves. She spends a few hours tending to others. Her thoughts are on Eddie. Breakfast of bread with a little bean is served. She enters Eddie's room with a plate of food in hand.

"Eat Eddie; this bread will give you strength and beans protein," as Maria walks to his bedside.

"How do you know my name?" Maria smiles as she moves a wooden chair closer to Eddie's bed. "Your dog tag."

He shakes his head, back and forth, refusing to eat. "I want to die. Leave me alone!"

"You will live Eddie, you must. Your wife awaits you in America."

"How do you know that I have a wife?" Maria sits next to Eddie holding bread and a glass of water. "You called her name as you slept."

"What would my wife want of me? I have no legs."

"I don't think that it will matter to your wife. You will live Eddie. You will get out of here and go on with your life's journey. I pray to God and say a daily rosary for you."

Eddie turns his head away from Maria.

"Leave me be."

Maria leaves Eddie's bedside with a heavy heart. She says to Eddie, "*Che cosa sarà sia-what will be will be.*"

Eddie looks away from the door, to stare at the dingy wall. Depression and despair encompass his being. He sobs for his mother. He cries for his wife. He yells in anguish over the loss of his limbs. He desires death. *I want none of this...death is welcomed.*

Maria's concern for this young American doesn't waver. She returns frequently to Eddie's bedside, speaking to him in Italian.

He doesn't eat for days. Fever is frequent, intermittently. Eddie's a lost being. He's void of eye contact with his caretaker. There's no conversation.

Maria tries another approach. She will not give up on Eddie. She speaks to him as a mother soothes her newborn. She sings Italian children songs. Maria hand feeds Eddie, now too weak to hold a spoon, his daily soup with some beans.

"Eddie, a friend of yours is going to join you in your room. You will share with him."

"I have no friends, Maria."

"Yes, you do."

"Who is he?"

"He will be moved a little bit later. Now rest. Sleep is good."

As Maria dims the light, Eddie stares at her, seeing Maria for the first time. Maria looks like his mother with her long wavy brown hair, tied in a bun. Those soft green eyes, her round pleasant face with gentleness makes her a guardian angel.

5

The noon hour comes. Eddie's sitting in bed awaiting the arrival of his friend. Maria appears at the doorway. "You ready?"

"Certo-of course!" A man with head bandages is rolled into Eddie's room. He stares at this injured soldier not quite knowing who he is. Eddie thinks that he looks vaguely familiar, however; with head bandages it's difficult to distinguish who it is. The soldier's brown eyes and engaging smile peer from bandages. "Eddie Bettino! It's me. I told you that I would come back for you, man."

Eddie smiles and his eyes instantly sparkle. "Your-um-Norman from the Bronx?"

Norman cries. Eddie tries to leave his bed to comfort his friend. Maria moves Norman's bed closer so that it's inches from Eddie. "Hey, Norman, it's alright, man."

"I'm so happy to see you again. I tried to return to you, Eddie. I failed you."

"No, you didn't fail me, Norman. It's life."

"But our life is going to be alright, isn't it? I mean we're going back home aren't we, Eddie."

"I'm hopeful that we will return home. We're prisoners of war, Norman."

"What will the Nazi's do with us? We're crippled. What will happen to us?"

"I don't know Norman."

Days come and go with injured troops entering the emergency hospital in critical condition. Many die. The days grow longer and Norman and Eddie continue to heal. Maria nurtures, feeds and tends to her charges. On Eddie's twentieth birthday she helps Eddie prepare a letter to his wife. The letter details why Eddie hasn't written and tells of his injuries.

"I will post your letter. I will make sure it gets from Italy. Your wife will receive this letter. She will wait for you."

"I am hopeful, Maria. Thank you for your help and caring for me."

"Enough sadness, this is your special day."

Maria leaves the room and returns. Norman yells and claps when he sees a candle lit cupcake arrive.

"Desiderio..."

"You want me to wish...freedom is what I wish for, Maria."

"Vive, Eddie."

Eddie smiles broadly as Norman begins to sing *Happy Birthday.* Eddie makes another wish this time silent and blows his candle out. Suddenly, German soldiers enter his room. With no words shared, Eddie's lifted and removed from his hospital room.

Maria cries out and holds her hands attempting to guard Eddie. Eddie looks at his cupcake. He looks to Norman.

Eddie's placed inside of a wagon. He sees the sun shining and hears birds chirping. Eddie views Italy's ravished countryside, on his twentieth birthday, on this twenty-seventh day of May.

The 45th Infantry Division, battered from conflict in Anzio, pushes slowly towards Rome arriving and liberating this war torn country on June 5, 1944. My nonno, his infantry division, is a distant memory, as he faces life as a prisoner. With a combination of limited medical treatment; poor diet; unbearable conditions within the stalag, life offers very little hope. I see my great-grandfather eating stale bread; sometimes-watery black bean or barley soup with an occasional piece of meat within the soup. Dysentery is frequent along with dehydration as he struggles to live.

I see great-grandfather sitting with others who hold their heads within their hands crying in anguish; some hearing voices from within. The injured with skeletal frames, hollow cheeks, and dark circles under muted eyes lie on dirty mats. I witness Nonno in poor health, body dirty, wearing soiled, and ill fitting clothing. He's weak; he has no strength to attempt escape. Life is bleak, there's hopelessness as the passage of days into the darkness of the nights pollutes his soul.

6

I observe Nana making parts for torpedoes. There's a picture of Nana and Nonno taped to her work place, a machine, in this General Motors factory. It's a photo of the couple, maybe on their honeymoon, or as high school sweethearts. They're sitting next to one another at the shore, both smiling with the vast ocean within reach.

Many women in this large windowless room are stuffed together like sardines within a can. Buses bring women, to the General Motors Plant, outside of Trenton to work. There's a shortage of men, and women work earning a living for their families. It's the war effort; patriotic women, building TBF Torpedo Bombers for Navy aircraft carriers. I see Nana standing in front of a machine, absent a smile.

Nana's stops rocking, shifts her weight and her rosary beads that I've been holding drop to the floor. In the distance I hear great-grandfather's voice, a tone of weakness. He's struggling. Nonno is sitting in a wheelchair; he's using his hands to manipulate the chair around an exercise area of the stalag. It's a hot day in early July. Great-grandfather's sweating and he's heading to a picnic table, located under a tree. There are International Red Cross provisions: some canned meat, canned fruit, bread and drinks. Nonno lowers his head, makes the Sign of the Cross, and begins to eat with others. Men from Australia, India, New Zealand and Britain sit together, as soldiers, united by circumstance.

It's the Fourth of July and Nana's standing on a sidewalk in front of the capital building waving a small American flag. Her mood is dark; with days of working, barely paying bills and carrying the burden of not knowing what's happened to her husband. She waves the American flag halfheartedly. She attempts a smile to grinning service men that have returned from overseas.

Nana's thoughts are doubtful. *Where's Eddie? Why hasn't he written?* She pulls a photo from her pocket. *I am angry. Why did you go to war? You have deserted me Eddie. I am alone. No husband, no children and barely enough energy to walk to the train station and wait for you. I stare at the scribble note that you wrote from basic training at Camp Dix. I want to rip this paper, toss it away but cannot as I have hope that you will return to me. This note is my life, and faith. The rose lady says, "Quasi mai." Is our life together almost never?*

The bleakness of total isolation encompasses the prisoners. No thoughts of escape enter Eddie's mind. He lacks strength and mobility. At night he prays and thinks of his wife. I watch as a fellow prisoner, a doctor, ambles to Nonno.

"I think I can help you walk again, Eddie."

"What can you do for me, doctor?"

"I know that I can design a pair of legs. There's some plaster. I could make a mold of each of your legs. I could put some steel rods in the mold and add a steel foot for you."

"Doctor, whatever you can do for me I would appreciate. I want to walk. I don't want my life as it is."

"I understand Eddie. Let me see what I can devise."

I view great-grandfather being fitted with a set of legs. He's smiling; his eyes happy, bright, and blue as the sky. I witness his first unsteady steps with the aid of two canes. He struggles with balance and muscular weakness. Pain and sweat bead his forehead. Soldiers stand encouraging and ready to render help for nonno in case he falls. He doesn't fall; he walks. Nonno sings; he cries with joy. Nonno thanks Saint Anthony and God.

The parade ends. Nana walks to South Clinton Avenue and enters the train station. The rose lady and shoeshine man are there. The shoeshine man's busy with a customer; the rose lady is feeding pigeons breadcrumbs. She stops her activity and walks to Nana.

"I didn't think that you would come today on the Fourth of July. Today we celebrate our freedom."

"I come every day. Today is as yesterday. Fourth of July is the same as every day. I did attend the parade."

"Have you heard from Eddie?"

"No, nothing...niente."

"How long will you wait."

"Forever."

"Quasi mai." The rose lady says scattering petals onto the tile floor. Nana nods her head as she walks away. Nana continues sitting. She stands for a few minutes. Nana opens her pocketbook, closes it. Nana sits again. Trains come and go. Her husband doesn't arrive.

7

July turns to August and September arrives. Leaves begin to change from green to gold and red. The daylight's shorter; nighttime's earlier, as World War II persists. The General Motors plant continues to build torpedo bombers. I see Nana weary. She doesn't visit Trenton Rail Station or attend Sunday mass. Many nights she cries herself to sleep.

September befalls October. The leaves gather on sidewalks as crisp winds blow foliage down walks and city streets. Pumpkins sit on porches as Halloween and Thanksgiving approach.

Eddie walks with purpose across the exercise yard. He enjoys practicing walking, demonstrating to comrades his gait, marveling by his new freedom. It's December and his captors meet with prisoners. The commander's speech is translated. He points to several men, one of which is my nonno. I move my head and strain my eyes trying to see and hear what's going on.

"You are a prisoner of war exchange with the Red Cross. You leave."

Without time for farewells, Eddie and other wounded leave the stalag and are transported to Annaburg, Germany. I see great-grandfather walking with the aid of artificial limbs and canes to a vehicle. He's transported to Geneva, Switzerland. Snow's covering the ground as he ambles onto a train, climbing its steps with help from other American soldiers. He enters the Port of Marseille, France and enjoys his first fresh fish stew since confinement.

Many soldiers board a Swedish ship, M.S. Gripsholm known as a "Mercy Ship". I stare as it leaves port with many wounded Americans bound for New York. Great-grandfather's standing on deck, slightly bent; grasping canes in both hands as brisk winds move his short brown hair.

Nana's walking home from the bus stop. She has worked twelve hours, is tired and cold. There's blustery weather in Trenton as wind blows around her. It zaps through her, catching the thin coat she's wearing, reaching her broken cold heart. It's dark, even though it's six in the evening. Walking to her front door, Nana notices a letter in her mailbox. *Perhaps correspondence from my Eddie?*

I stare at my great-grandmother. I wonder what this letter is about. I view Nana as she grabs the letter. She strains her eyes to see the postmark. Nana's unable to see the writing. She quickly unlocks her door, turns on the nearest light dropping her pocketbook to the floor. Nana breathes deeply. Tears form within her eyes as she opens the letter. It's dated, March 1944. I observe Nana as her mouth opens. Clutching the letter, she falls to the floor, holding it to her heart. On her knees she rocks, back and forth; Nana screams.

Eddie grows in mind and strength while medical doctors assess and medically treat him. I observe great-grandfather mingling with comrades, those who have lost limbs, those who have lost their minds somewhere on European battlefields. I feel his inner spirit and see his tender eyes. A slightly built man walks to Eddie.

"My friend...I can't believe it's you!"

"Eddie turns and smiles. Norman! You made it out of Italy."

"Yes, Eddie. As you, I went to a stalag, almost died from my head injuries."

"Enough talk about the past."

"I know the past is painful. We're here and we're going home man!" Norman says smiling boldly and holding onto great-grandfather.

The men stand on deck with the sun on their faces and wind in their hair. Norman takes Eddie's warm hands. "I told you man that I would return for you. I tried hard Eddie; I feel that I let you down."

"Norman, I knew when I was hit that I might not survive. I thank you for carrying me and spending time with me. I will never forget you, my friend."

They embrace.

8

I look over my shoulder and gaze at Nana. She's in the kitchen and a pot of water is boiling on the range. There's a woman sitting at the kitchen table reading the letter from Eddie. The woman cries, and removes herself from the table. She leaves the kitchen without taking the letter.

Nana retrieves her cracked blue mug from the cabinet and pours boiling water into it. A tea bag floats within. "Mom, please return to the kitchen. I made you a cup of tea. I need you."

Nana's mother comes into the kitchen. She's holding her confirmation rosary. Nana walks over to her mother, kisses her cheek.

"Mom, I need to know if Eddie's alive. Where he is? I can't go on like this."

"Certo...certainly, I understand."

"I want my husband back...alive...or dead, with or without legs. I can't live."

"We must have faith and hope."

"I'm done with faith and have little hope left."

Eddie stands on deck with men who have become his friends. All watch as the sight of the Statute of Liberty merges with this peaceful day. Sea gulls fly overhead as the M.S. Gripsholm is lead to port in New York City. Men hail, cheer and cry. Norman stands next to Eddie.

"We've made it!" says Charlie from Jersey City.

"I'm going home!" Al from Boston says.

Ricky from New Haven says a silent prayer. "Let's kiss the ground when we get off" says Ben as he pats Eddie on the back and shakes Norman's hand.

Nonno stares at the Statute of Liberty; the sun is shining behind it as the M.S. Gripsholm passes. Nonno looks at the sun and takes deep breaths as he breathes salty cold air. It's a frosty day in the city as

Eddie's helped off deck. Norman follows closely.

"Eddie, this is probably the last time that we will be together, man. If you ever come to the Bronx, look me up. Here's my address. I wish you the best."

Tears form within the men's eyes as they shake hands and hug. "I will not forget how you helped me. I think if you hadn't left me where you did, I would not be here today."

"We need to put what happened in Italy away somewhere, man. I don't know where the hell to put it, but somewhere."

"You're right, Norman. I plan to see my wife as soon as I get to New Jersey."

"You do that man. I will never forget you."

Eddie is ushered to a nearby bus. He moves slowly. He takes a moment to look at the harbor and sees Norman's back. He's walking earnestly.

Eddie's transported to nearby Halloran Hospital and within hours leaves New York for Atlantic City.   There's a hospital on Atlantic City's Boardwalk, close to home. He's anxious to find a way to Trenton.

Nana walks to West State Street from her apartment. It's about a thirty-minute walk. There's determination in her steps. I study her. Nana's shoulders are back, head's up and eyes fixed. I see her stop, open her pocketbook and take a letter from it. It's Eddie's correspondence; I can see my great-grandfather's handwriting. Nana places the letter back into her bag. She continues forward with strength of mind.

Eddie's arrival at Thomas M. England General Hospital is marked with trepidation. Within his mind he has devised a plan to visit his wife. Since Nancy doesn't have a telephone, he will travel by train, and surprise her. Eddie's concerned as to how he looks. He's twenty, and although steadily gaining some weight and muscle, he looks pale and bony. *Will she still love me? I was a prisoner of war for thirteen months, what will she think of that? Has she waited for me these two years? I have no legs...*

Negative thoughts mixed with doubt encompass Eddie's mind making him skeptical of his plan. Eddie's attention is diverted when a doctor and nurse enter the examination room.

"Edward Bettino. I would like to introduce myself. I'm Doctor Melvin Smith, a surgeon and this is Nurse Sarah Tucker. I have been reviewing your medical information from the Gripsholm. I'd like to complete an examination of your legs."

Eddie slides his pants down and undoes his artificial legs. The doctor and nurse stare at his primitive amputation. The nurse checks vitals. The doctor looks away and down at the floor.

"It is with regret that I tell you that your legs will need to be re-amputated. You need to be fitted properly and of course with the latest modern prostheses. Once healed, you'll walk with comfort and without the aid of canes."

Eddie looks down at his stumps. For a moment in time he's unable to catch his breath. He digests his medical prognosis. He shakes his head, as though he's hearing voices. Perhaps doubt and despair continues within his mind. "Doctor Smith, I need to go to Trenton for a day or two before doing this. I have a wife that I haven't seen in almost two years."

Doctor Smith and the nurse look at one another. The doctor scratches his head. "I see, Eddie and understand. You will be given a three-day pass. There's a social worker who can help you plan this and fund your travels. It will take a minute for me to complete your furlough information for Social Worker Ginny Quinton."

9

Nana sits on a bench at the State House for over an hour. Nobody's giving her attention, although she's been assured by the secretary upon arrival that she would be spoken with today. Employees scurry about their business. She begins a ritual of self-doubt. *Perhaps I shouldn't have come. Everybody is too busy. Why would the congressman agree to speak with me?* She waits, sitting patiently. She hears the secretary's desk phone ring and observes the secretary looking in her direction. The secretary calls her name. Nana stands.

"Please follow me, Mrs. Bettino."

Nana totes her pocketbook, holding it closely to her side and follows. She enters the congressman's office. He's sitting behind his desk. When Congressman Mathews sees my great-grandmother, he stands to greet her. He motions for Nana to take a seat and resumes sitting behind his desk.

"How can I be of service for you; Mrs. Bettino."

Nana stares at the window to the rear of the office. There are barren trees and gray sky. *I feel as barren as the trees and dark as the sky.*

Nana stands to address Congressman Mathews. "My name is Nancy Bettino and I'm here because I want to know what happened to my husband." She hands Congressman Mathews her husband's correspondence. She returns to her seat, sits and stares fidgeting; her hands folded, thumbs moving in circles on top of her pocketbook.

Congressman Mathews places his glasses on the desk, wipes his eyes and forehead. He looks into Nana's eyes. "I am very sorry."

"I want my Eddie back. If he's dead, I want his body found and returned to me. Enough already."

"I understand how you are feeling."

"Sir, I don't think that you understand my feeling. Eddie and I have been together since Trenton High School days, high school sweethearts. We married upon graduation as Eddie was drafted directly thereafter. Our youth is gone. I have endured two years without him. I live day-to-day dreaming of the past. My life is nothing without him. If he hasn't survived, I want his remains. I want him to have a proper burial. I want him back!"

Congressman Mathews pushes his chair back, stands and walks to Nana. "Do you have a number where I may reach you?"

Nana hands the congressman a number on a small piece of paper. "This is my mother's number. She will deliver any messages to me."

"Nancy, give me a few days and I will get back with you."

Multicolored rose petals swirl on Trenton's Rail Station's black and white tile floor. The rose lady's throwing breadcrumbs to pigeons when Nana enters the station. Her eyes are swollen from crying as she walks to a crowded bench. Nana squeezes to sit alongside of a child. She looks at the little girl with blond curly hair and blue eyes and smiles. The rose lady and shoeshine man walk over to her.

"We haven't seen you in awhile."

"I know."

"Where have you been?"

"Nowhere."

The shoeshine man stands in front of Nana. "Would you like for me to shine your shoes?"

"My husband has no legs...he's a prisoner of war...no shoes to shine."

The rose lady pats Nana on her back. "We didn't know. We're sorry."

"Enough is enough, I told our congressman."

The rose lady pats Nana on her back, "Quasi mai."

A train arrives at the station. Nana opens her pocketbook removing a piece of folded paper. Soldiers arrive and walk into the lobby. The rose lady and shoeshine man watch. A soldier slowly walks emerging from the platform. He's holding two canes one in each hand, slightly bent over. This soldier pauses staring towards the crowded bench, taking a moment to catch his breath from the physical exertion of walking up a stairway from the platform. I see Nana look in his direction. Crystal blue eyes greet her with a smile, that's a little bit off center. There's a slightly crooked nose, broken from boxing. He looks to my Nana. She shouts running and screaming across the lobby. Pigeons take flight. Rose petals swirl. The rose lady and shoeshine man stare in awe.

"Eddie, my God...Eddie you've returned. My God...thank you." There are tears of joy-tears of hope-and tears of love as they embrace.

They pull apart and stare. They smile and kiss. They hold each other wanting eternity.

The shoeshine man walks over to Eddie, pats his back and shakes great-grandfather's hand. The rose lady is close behind, she hands Eddie a red rose. "God Bless you." She says.

Nana stops rocking. We awaken. The sun's shining and I hear neighbors talking and children playing kick ball in the middle of Columbus Avenue.

"Nana, what does the yellow piece of paper say that you hold?"

"My grandson, this piece of paper was written by your great-grandfather while he was in the Army. He spent time at Camp Dix. Nana was not happy that her husband was a soldier. I have held this piece of paper for many years and have read it many times. I read it to remind me of life."

"So what does it say, Nana?"

"It says... *War is not pleasant but I did what was expected of me...did my duty along with hundreds of others.*"

"I love you Nana."

"I love you, my grandson. Are you hungry?"

"Yes, Nana. Can you make Pork Roll? It will make me feel better to eat a Pork Roll sandwich."

"You are like your great-grandfather. It was his favorite sandwich."

I look at the Crown of Thorns, its moist leaves and branches reaching outward; perhaps to heaven where great-grandfather lives. Nana's rosary is sitting on the floor. She carries her piece of paper in hand as we walk to the kitchen. Nana starts a pot for tea on the stove. She takes an iron skillet from the oven placing it onto the range. She starts frying some Trenton Pork Roll.

The water boils as she places a tea bag in the pot. Nana ambles to the nearby cabinet and gets two mugs. One's a blue cracked mug. Sandwiches are made as tea is poured. A pot of gravy, with some sausage is simmering on the stove for tonight's meal.

"Nana, what do you want to do after lunch?"

"How about a game of cards?"

"Can we play Old Maids?"

"Certo...my grandson."

And I smile, and think of nonno. I say under my breath...*quasi mai*...almost never.

Epilogue

My father, Edward Thomas Bettino, was born to Adele and Delespro Bettino, in Ogdensburg, New Jersey on May 27, 1924. Albert Bettino my father's older brother a paratrooper was shot and killed in Belgium during the Battle of the Bulge in December 1944. My father has a younger brother, Joseph who was born after the sudden death of my grandfather at the age of 36. Our grandmother, Adele remarried and produced three children, Frances and twins Rose and Rosario Gondolfo.

My mother, Nancy Mumola met and fell in love with my father after the war. Dad had secured an administrative position in Trenton with the Department of Labor, where my mother was employed. She told me many years ago; "I fell in love with your father the moment he walked into the office where I was working...I fell in love with his blue eyes!"

Three children were born to this union: my sister, Celeste, me, Teresa, and my brother, Edward.

My parents have four grandchildren: Andrew Bettino, Daniel Bettino, Grace Bettino and Joseph Green. A great-grandchild, Ansel Edward Bettino was born on July 19, 2012.

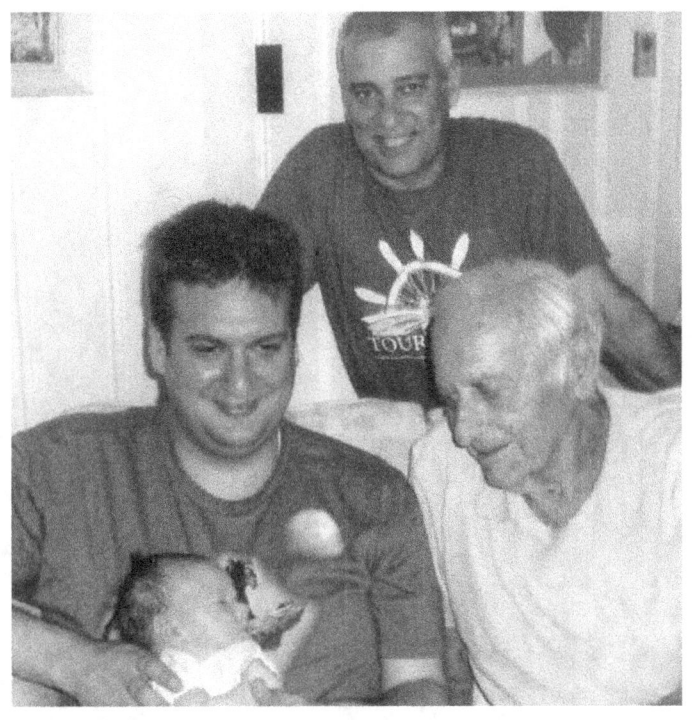

Photo: Four Generations (Right to Left)
Edward Sr., Edward Thomas, Andrew
Edward (holding Ansel Edward)

Books by Teresa Adele Bettino

The Adventures of Sugarbabe and Thunder

The Ten Commandments of a Welfare Worker

Degen and Me

The Cats of Hanover Juvenile Correctional Center

Unique Shadows

A Wicker Rocker

Two Dogs and a Boy

Wind Chimes

Jigsaw

Ed and Nancy Bettino Wedding Photo 1950

This Page Intentionally Blank